The Red-Headed League

By Arthur Conan Doyle

Adapted by David Eastman

Illustrated by Allan Eitzen

TROLL ASSOCIATES

Library of Congress Cataloging in Publication Data

Eastman, David.
    Sherlock Holmes—The red-headed league.

    Summary: A suspicious new member solicits the
aid of Sherlock Holmes in uncovering the secret
behind the Red-Headed League.
    [1. Mystery and detective stories] I. Doyle,
Arthur Conan, Sir, 1859-1930. Red-headed league.
II. Eitzen, Allan, ill. III. Title.
PZ7.E1269Re   [Fic]   81-11619
ISBN 0-89375-614-8   AACR2
ISBN 0-89375-615-6 (pbk.)

Printed in the United States of America
10 9 8 7 6 5 4 3 2 1

When I called at the Baker Street offices of my friend, Mr. Sherlock Holmes, I found that he was not alone. With him was a fat red-haired man, who was searching through an old newspaper. Holmes said, "Ah, come in, Dr. Watson. This is Mr. Wilson. He has just begun what promises to be a very strange tale."

3

Mr. Wilson's appearance told me nothing about him. But Holmes was an expert at observation and deduction. He announced, "Mr. Wilson once worked with his hands, he is a Freemason, he has been to China, and he has done quite a bit of writing lately."

"How on earth did you know all that?" asked Wilson in astonishment.

"Your right hand is larger than your left because you have worked more with it," explained Holmes. "You wear the pin of the Freemasons. That tattoo on your wrist could only have been made in China, and you have a Chinese coin hanging from your watch chain. Moreover, your right cuff is shiny where it has rubbed against the writing table."

"Remarkable," I said.

"Ah, here it is," said Wilson. "This is what started it all, two months ago." He showed us the following advertisement:

There is now a vacancy in the Red-Headed League. This position requires little work, and the member will earn a large salary. All red-headed men are eligible. Apply at 7 Pope's Court, Fleet Street.

"My assistant at the pawnshop found the advertisement," explained Mr. Wilson. "His name is Vincent Spaulding. He is very bright. And he is also willing to work for low wages, while he learns the business. Oh, he has his faults—he is always diving down into the cellar to develop his photographs—but he is a good worker.

"At any rate," continued Mr. Wilson, "he thought I ought to apply for the position. He had heard that a man with a fiery head of red hair—like mine—stood a better chance. So we closed the shop and went to the address given in the advertisement. The street was crowded with red-headed men!

"Well, Mr. Spaulding pushed and pulled and bullied until he got me through the crowd. We reached some steps, which led up to an office. There were two lines of people—one going up hopefully, and one coming back sadly. We squeezed into the hopeful line, and soon we were inside the office.

"A red-headed man behind a desk looked at me, cocked his head to one side, and stared at my hair until I felt quite bashful. Then he grabbed my hair with both hands and tugged until my eyes began to water. Then he congratulated me, stuck his head outside, and announced that the vacancy had been filled.

"The only conditions were that I must stay in that office from ten o'clock until two each day and copy from the encyclopedia. For this, I was to receive a very good salary. My assistant could certainly mind the pawnshop for four hours a day! So I accepted the job.

"I reported at ten o'clock the next morning. The red-headed man was there, and he started me off with the letter A. He looked in on me from time to time and returned at two o'clock. Before I left for the day, he complimented me on the amount I had written. Then he closed and locked the door.

"This went on for eight weeks. I was paid each Saturday. After a while, the red-headed man stopped coming. But I still reported from ten till two and picked up my pay each week. Then today, I found a sign nailed to the door. It said: THE RED-HEADED LEAGUE IS ENDED. *OCTOBER 9, 1890.*"

THE
RED-HEADED
LEAGUE
IS ENDED.
OCTOBER
9,
1890

"What did you do when you found the note?" asked Holmes.

"I went to the landlord," replied Mr. Wilson. "He said that the red-headed gentleman had moved. I went to his new address, but it turned out to be a company that makes artificial kneecaps. So I decided to come to you."

14

When our visitor left, Holmes said, "Well, Watson, what do you make of it?"

"I make nothing of it," I answered. "It is a most mysterious business."

"The more unusual a thing is, the less mysterious it proves to be," replied Holmes. "I must think about this for a while." Then he lit his pipe and closed his eyes.

Suddenly, my friend sprang out of his chair as if he had made up his mind about something. He said, "If you have a few hours to spare, Watson, put on your hat, and come along."

Before long, we stood in front of Mr. Wilson's house. Holmes studied it carefully. Downstairs was the pawnshop. Upstairs was the pawnbroker's residence.

He walked up to the shop and knocked. A bright-looking young man opened the door.

"Good morning," said Holmes. "Can you direct me to the beach?"

"Third right, fourth left," answered the young man. Then he went back inside and closed the door.

"I trust you asked directions only so you could see the pawnbroker's assistant," I said.

"Not to see *him*," replied Holmes, "but to see the knees of his trousers."

"And what did you see?" I asked.

"What I expected to see," said Holmes. "But this is a time for observation, not for talk. Let us see what is on the next street."

The busy street behind the pawnshop was lined with shops and businesses—the tobacco store, the newspaper shop, the City and Suburban Bank, the Vegetarian Restaurant, and McFarlane's carriage-building warehouse.

"A crime is being planned," announced Holmes, "but we can stop it. Meet me at Baker Street at ten tonight. And bring your revolver." Then he turned and disappeared.

I am no more dense than my neighbors, but I always feel very stupid when I am around Sherlock Holmes. Each of us had heard and seen the same things. Yet he saw clearly what was about to happen, while I was totally mystified. That night, when I joined Holmes at his Baker Street office, I found two other men there.

I recognized Peter Jones of the police, and Holmes introduced the other man as Mr. Merryweather.

"We are playing for high stakes," said Holmes. "For you, Mr. Merryweather, the prize will be a fortune in gold. For Mr. Jones, it will be John Clay—murderer, thief, and forger. Now, gentlemen, we must be off."

Jones and Merryweather rode in one carriage, while Holmes and I rode in another. We rattled through an endless maze of gas-lit streets. At last, Holmes said, "This fellow Merryweather is the director of the City and Suburban Bank. Our friend Officer Jones is a complete idiot in his profession, but he is as brave as a bulldog. Well, here we are."

It was the same busy street on which we had stood that morning. Mr. Merryweather led us down a narrow passage and opened a side door. Inside, there was a gate and a flight of stone steps that led to another gate. We went through another door and entered a huge cellar, which was filled with crates and boxes.

"You are well protected above," Holmes remarked.

"And below," added Merryweather, striking his stick on the flagstone floor. "Why, dear me! It sounds quite hollow." He looked up in surprise.

"Please be more quiet," scolded Holmes, "or you will spoil everything!" Then he took out his magnifying glass and fell to his knees, examining the cracks between the flagstones.

"They cannot begin before the pawnbroker is asleep, so we must wait," said Holmes. "As you may have guessed, Watson, we are in the cellar of the City and Suburban Bank. In these crates is a fortune in French gold. Some of the most daring criminals in London will try to steal it tonight.

"We will have to wait in the dark," continued Holmes. "When I flash a light on the thieves, close in quickly. If they fire, Watson, do not hesitate to shoot them down."

I placed my revolver on a wooden crate in front of me. Then we waited in complete darkness.

"Their only retreat is back through the pawnbroker's shop,"
whispered Holmes. "Have you done what I asked, Mr. Jones?"

Jones replied, "An inspector and two officers are waiting
there."

We waited for over an hour. Each minute seemed an hour,
and every muscle in my body was tense. Suddenly, I saw a thin
beam of light coming from the middle of the floor!

A cracking sound filled the cellar, and one of the flagstones was raised. Lantern light streamed up through the large hole. Then the pawnbroker's assistant climbed up, followed by a red-headed man.

"It's all clear," whispered the assistant. "Do you have the chisel and the bags?" Then he gave a startled cry. "Great Scott! Run for it!"

Sherlock Holmes seized the intruder by the collar. Knocking a gun from the man's hand, he said, "It's no use, John Clay— I've got you. And there are three men waiting for your friend at the pawnbroker's door." Jones snapped a pair of handcuffs on the criminal and marched him out.

"Really, Mr. Holmes," said Mr. Merryweather as we left the cellar. "If it had not been for you, the bank would have been empty before morning. How can we ever repay you?"

"Naturally, I expect the bank to pay my expenses," said Holmes. "But my real reward has been hearing the very unusual tale of the Red-Headed League."

Back at Baker Street, Holmes remarked, "The purpose of the Red-Headed League was to get the pawnbroker out of his shop. I suspected the assistant, because he worked for low wages and kept disappearing into the cellar. His dirty trouser knees meant that he was digging a tunnel. But where did it lead?

"When I saw that the bank was on the street behind the pawnshop, the mystery was all but solved. The League had ended because the tunnel was finished. That meant the robbery would take place soon. And today is Saturday—the perfect day for a bank robbery."

"Remarkable, Mr. Holmes," said I.

"Elementary, my dear Watson," replied Holmes.